My Cat Pearl

For my mother, Claire

Copyright © 1980 by Dona M. Turner
All rights reserved. Printed in the United States of America.
Designed by Trish Parcell

Library of Congress Cataloging in Publication Data
Turner, Dona.
   My cat Pearl.
   SUMMARY: Describes the everyday activities of a pet
cat and her young mistress.
   1. Cats—Legends and stories. [1. Cats—Fiction]
I. Title.
PZ10.3.T8925My 1979   [E]   79-7402
ISBN 0-690-03989-1
ISBN 0-690-03990-5 lib. bdg.

10 9 8 7 6 5 4 3 2 1
First Edition

My Cat Pearl

by Dona Turner

T.Y. CROWELL · NEW YORK

Every morning when

I wake up there is

something in my bed.

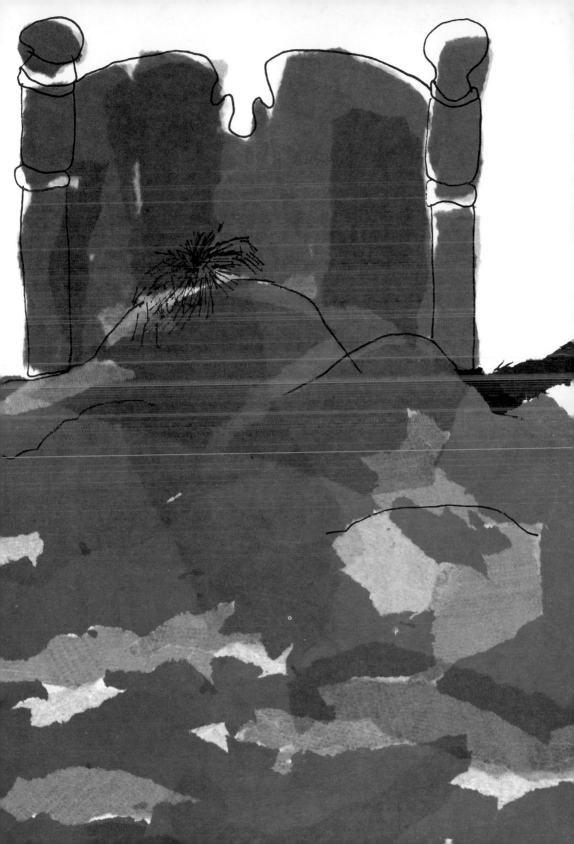

I pull down

the covers

and there is

Pearl.

She follows me

to the bathroom,

she follows me

to the kitchen,

where I give

her breakfast.

She goes outside,

then comes in again.

She watches
while I find
my clothes,

and tries to
sneak out
past me
when I leave
the house.

She sleeps all day,

curled in a chair,

or

on the bookcase,

or

in the

kitchen

cabinet,

or

under

the couch.

When I come home

from school,

I chase her around.

Then she hides and

waits for me to

find her.

When I do,

she jumps high

in the air.

She likes to

chase a little fish

made out of leather

and tied on a string,

or climb into

paper bags.

Sometimes when I go

to bed at night she

stays up late and

visits friends.

But,

every morning when

I wake up there is

something in my bed.

I pull down

the covers

and there is

my Pearl.